The Little Auto

THE
LITTLE
AUTO

LOIS LENSKI

Random House New York

Mr. Small has a
little Auto. It is red
and shiny. He likes
to look at it.

Mr. Small keeps
the little Auto in the
garage at the end of
the driveway.

Mr. Small has
overalls on. He
is oiling the little
Auto.

The little Auto has
rubber tires. Mr. Small
is pumping them up.

The little Auto has
a radiator. Mr. Small
is filling it with water.

It is a fine day.
Mr. Small is going
for a drive. He steps
on the starter. The
engine begins to hum.

The little Auto
backs out of the
garage. It goes
chug-chug down
the driveway.

The little Auto
goes down the road.
Mr. Small toots the
horn. *Beep, beep!*
He scares the ducks
and chickens.

A small dog follows
the little Auto, but is
soon left far behind.

The little Auto
is going fast. It
passes a horse
and buggy.

The little Auto
goes UPHILL

and the little Auto
goes DOWNHILL!

The little Auto
comes to town.
Mr. Small drives
down the right
side of the street.

The little Auto comes
to a STOP-GO sign and
waits for the policeman
to turn it.

The little Auto goes
down MAIN STREET.

The little Auto
stops at a Filling
Station. Mr. Small
buys five gallons
of gas.

The little Auto
catches up with
a Trolley Car. It
waits for the
people to get off.

Mr. Small parks
the little Auto in
front of a store.
He is going in to
buy a newspaper.

The little Auto
starts for home.
It comes to a red
light and waits for
it to turn green.

On the way home
it begins to rain. Mr.
Small has to put the
top up so he won't
get wet.

Pop!
Mr. Small
has a flat tire!

Mr. Small jacks the little Auto up. He puts on the spare tire. And then the sun comes out!

Soon the little Auto is back in the garage. After it is washed and polished, it shines like new.

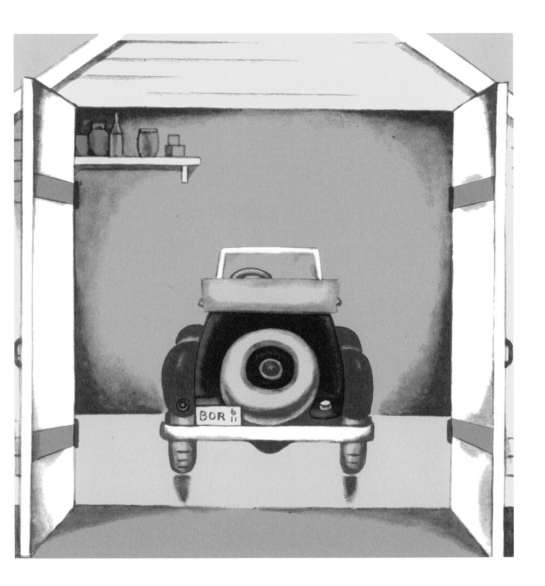

and
that's all!